FLUTTERBY FLY

Written by Stephen Cosgrove
Illustrated by Robin James

A Serendipity™ *Book*

D1315320

PSS!
PRICE STERN SLOAN

The Serendipity™ series was created by Stephen Cosgrove and Robin James

Copyright © 1984, 2001 by Price Stern Sloan. All rights reserved.
Published by Price Stern Sloan, a division of
Penguin Putnam Books for Young Readers, New York.

ISBN 0-8431-2001-0

2001 Revised Edition
2004 Printing

PSS! is a registered trademark of Penguin Putnam Inc.
Serendipity and the pink dragon are trademarks of Penguin Putnam Inc.

Dedicated to the memory
of the real Flutterby.
She died too soon ever to be able to fly.

– Stephen

Far beyond the horizon, in the middle of the Crystal Sea is a magical island that is known as Serendipity. On the island, nestled in the foothills of Crystal Mountain, just below where feathery wisps of mists begin to call themselves clouds, is a small valley called WingSong.

Here blossoms and leaves seem to sigh as they flutter on breezes up to the sky.

It was odd, but at times the trees appeared to lose all their leaves as the breeze whipped about the meadow. But it is said that appearances can be deceiving, for these were not leaves at all – these were butterflies, hundreds and hundreds of butterflies that flittered and fluttered about.

Have you ever wondered where the butterflies go when summer turns to winter turns to fall? Have you ever wondered, as have I?

Well, wonder no more. For they come here, to the Valley of WingSong, on the Island of Serendipity.

Here in WingSong they live forever gathered together in butterfly clouds of a hundred or more. Here they were gently herded from one place to another by tiny, winged horses called FlutterFlies. The FlutterFlies would flap their wings and fly about WingSong guiding clouds of butterflies from bush to flower to tree.

One such FlutterFly was called FlutterBy, and truly, how she could fly! She would dip and soar on the smallest of breezes chasing after any butterfly that had flittered away from the safety of the cloud. If a butterfly became lost, FlutterBy would kick her heels and flap her wings and swoop down and guide the little butterfly back to safety.

One day, as FlutterBy was guiding her cloud of butterflies near the forest of scented cedar and pine she heard the butterflies anxiously whispering to one another. The whispering became louder and louder. The louder the whispering, the faster the butterflies flapped their wings. One minute there was an organized cloud of butterflies, and in the next minute butterflies were flying in different directions—like a rainbow exploding into hundreds of pieces.

FlutterBy did as she had been trained, flying this way and that, settling the butterflies and drawing them back into an organized cloud.

When the cloud was settled again and all the butterflies were flying in the same direction, FlutterBy asked, "What happened? Who said what to whom that caused you to fly all over the sky?"

The butterflies were still a bit skitterish but finally one of them flapped near to the little winged horse and whispered, "We heard horrible gossip on the wind."

"What gossip?" she asked.

"Well, this is what I heard," the butterfly whispered in her ear. "Ugly, ugly butterfly. Fly away or you shall die!"

FlutterBy reared back in shock. "Who would say such a thing?" she whinnied.

"Well," said the butterfly, arching its antennae, "I shouldn't tell you, but . . . well, it was the old black crow that lives in the bracken in the wood."

FlutterBy settled the cloud of butterflies above a purple lilac bush, and then went off in search of the old black crow. She flew to the bracken in the wood and there, sure enough, she found the old black crow.

FlutterBy was very, very angry about what had happened and tersely asked, "Why did you say what you said? 'Ugly, ugly butterfly. Fly away or you shall die!' Why would you say such a thing?"

"Naw! Naw!" cawed the crow. "They heard me wrong. I never said such a thing. What I told them was exactly what I had heard which was, 'Don't sigh, butterfly. Fly away or you shall cry!' That was it."

"That's almost as bad," muttered FlutterBy. "Who would say such a thing?"

"Well," crowed the crow in a gossipy way sidestepping on the branch, "it was a secret, and well, I promised not to tell, but, since you asked, it was that chubby little chipmunk that lives in the old tree by the well."

"Then I shall have a talk with this gossipy little creature," said FlutterBy as she flew away. "I will put an end to this, once and for all."

She flew deep into the forest until she came to the old tree that stood beside the well. Just as the crow had cawed, there was the chipmunk, chattering away to anyone and everyone that would listen.

"Hey, hey, hello," the chipmunk chattered. "Light down a spell. I have many, many stories to tell."

FlutterBy fluttered down to a branch, and with her hooves clicking on the bark of the wood she asked sternly, "Are you the source of all this gossip. Are you the one who told the crow 'Don't sigh, butterfly. Fly away or you shall cry?' Why would you say such a thing?"

"Hey, hey, little FlutterFly, I didn't say that. No, sirree!" he said as he scooted closer and arched his brow. "I said that I had heard: 'Better fly, butterfly. Fly away and don't you lie.' That's what I heard. That's what I said."

"Who would say such a thing?" asked FlutterBy.

"Well, I promised not to tell, but since you asked, it was the old monarch butterfly that lives down in the gnarled branches just above the well."

FlutterBy stomped her foot in anger and then lifted off the branch and fluttered down to the well. There in the gnarled twisted branches she found the old butterfly basking in a warm shaft of sunlight from the sky overhead.

FlutterBy stood there for a moment staring at the old butterfly and then sternly asked, "Are you the butterfly that told the chipmunk, who told the crow, who told my cloud of butterflies, 'Better fly, butterfly. Fly away and don't you lie?' Why would you say such a thing?"

The old butterfly leaned back, clapping his hands. "Not I," said he. "I would never say such a thing. But I do call to all the new butterflies that come to Island of Serendipity. I tell one and all: Fly so high, butterfly. Fly away and touch the sky!"

"Oh, dear," sighed FlutterBy, "this all been nothing but a game of gossip." She thanked the old butterfly for his time and then flew back to her cloud of butterflies which were still hovering about the purple lilac bush.

She fluttered down into the cloud and spoke loudly so that all could hear, "Listen little butterflies. There is and was nothing to fear. What you heard before was only gossip, nearly lies."

All of the butterflies nodded their heads in understanding.

Satisfied that all was well, FlutterBy herded the cloud of butterflies to the other end of WingSong where the sweet clover grew.

To the back of the cloud you could hear voices muttering and mumbling.

"What did she say?"

"I don't know. I think FlutterBy said something about moaning warships and dearly sighs."

"Oh, no! Did you hear that?" said one to another, "FlutterBy is glued to a bug strip and now she can't fly!"

GOSSIP GARBLES VERY WELL

ALL THE THINGS YOU WANT TO TELL

SO, IF YOU HEAR SOME GOSSIP TRUE

LET THE GOSSIP STOP WITH YOU!

Serendipity™ Books

Created by
Stephen Cosgrove and Robin James

Enjoy all the delightful books in the Serendipity™ Series:

Available wherever books are sold.

PSS!
PRICE STERN SLOAN